Rainbows
for
Jacque!

George
Ella
Lyon

2001

COME A TIDE

Story by George Ella Lyon

Pictures by Stephen Gammell

ORCHARD BOOKS · NEW YORK

For friends and neighbors
in Harlan County, Kentucky
and for everyone who ever dug out

G.E.L.

*L*ast March it snowed
and then it rained
for four days and nights.

"It'll come a tide,"
my grandma said.

And sure enough,
when all the creeks
rushed down to the river
like kinfolks coming home,

it did.

It washed away
little naked gardens
on Clover Fork

pigs and chickens
on Martins Fork

and a whole front porch
on Poor Fork.

We stood on our bridge
and watched them swirl by.
Ooo-eee! Ooo-eee! cried the pigs.
The river nudged the bridge bottom.

Still we boasted,
"It won't flood us."

But we left our radios crackling
that night when we went to sleep.

The warning whistle
didn't have to blow twice.

Cloudburst! the radio said.
Wall of water coming down!

In five minutes
we'd jumped in our clothes
and were outside headed for the truck.

"Did you hear the whistle?
Do you want to go with us?"
Mama called to our neighbor, Mrs. Mac.

"Joe won't go
till he finds his teeth
so I've put a pot of coffee on."

"Did you hear the whistle?
Do you want to go with us?"
Mama called to the Cains across the street.

"I can't catch Donald!" John yelled back.

"It's that duck," his mother hollered.
"John has to save the one thing that swims.
Don't stall on our account."

"Did you hear the whistle?
Do you want to go with us?"
Mama called to Papa Bill next door.

"I heard it, honey.
But I've got me a boat
and I'm aiming to find the oars."

She fed us warmed-over biscuits
and coffee stout as a post.
Then she sent us to bed.

Rain came down like curtains
as we drove up Grandma's hill.

When light flooded in
and I was asleep,
Daddy went out scouting.

"Water up to the piano keys
but the house is solid."

"What do we do now?"

"If it was me," Grandma said,
"I'd make friends with a shovel."

And we did.

The Macs, the Cains, Papa Bill:
next day everyone was shoveling.
Soggy furniture and mud-mapped rugs
made mountains in front of each house.

"It got us this time,"
we had to admit,
taking lunch at the rescue wagon.

But we dug and hauled,
we scrubbed and crawled
to find our buried treasure.

Now we'll be fine,
except in spring
when the snow and rain
come together.

Then I'll hold my breath
and hope Grandma won't say,
"Children, it'll come a tide."

Text copyright © 1990 by George Ella Lyon
Illustrations copyright © 1990 by Stephen Gammell
First Orchard Paperbacks edition 1993

Orchard Books
95 Madison Avenue, New York, NY 10016

Manufactured in the United States of America. Book design
by Mina Greenstein.   The text of this book is set in 16 pt.
ITC Bookman Light. The illustrations are colored pencil
and watercolor drawings, reproduced in halftone.
10 9 8 7 6 5 4 3

Library of Congress Cataloging-in-Publication Data
Lyon, George Ella, date.   Come a tide / by George Ella Lyon;
illustrated by Stephen Gammell.   p.   cm.   "A Richard
Jackson book"— Summary: A girl provides a lighthearted
account of the spring floods at her rural home.
ISBN 0-531-05854-9 (tr.) ISBN 0-531-08454-X (lib. bdg.)
ISBN 0-531-07036-0 (pbk.)
[1. Floods—Fiction. 2. Country Life—Fiction.] I.
Gammell, Stephen, ill. II. Title. PZ7.L9954Co 1990
[E]—dc20   88-35650